This story is based on the traditional Aesop fable,
The Boy Who Cried Wolf, but with a new twist.
You can read the original story in
Must Know Stories. Can you make
up your own twist for the story?

Franklin Watts
First published in great Britain in 2015 by The Watts Publishing Group

Text © Laura North 2015
Illustrations © Becka Moor 2015

The rights of Laura North to be identified as the author
and Becka Moor as the illustrator of this Work have been asserted
in accordance with the Copyright, Designs and Patents Act, 1988.

ISBN 978 1 4451 4291 3 (hbk)
ISBN 978 1 4451 4292 0 (pbk)
ISBN 978 1 4451 4294 4 (library ebook)

Series Editor: Melanie Palmer
Series Advisor: Catherine Glavina
Series Designer: Peter Scoulding
Cover Designer: Cathyrn Gilbert

Printed in China

Franklin Watts
An imprint of
Hachette Children's Group
Part of The Watts Publishing Group
Carmelite House
50 Victoria Embankment
London EC4Y 0DZ

An Hachette UK Company
www.hachette.co.uk

www.franklinwatts.co.uk

MIX
Paper from
responsible sources
FSC® C104740
FSC
www.fsc.org

A young shepherd boy lived at the
edge of a big forest full of wolves.

Every day, he walked through
the forest with a girl who wore
a little red hood. She was terrified
of wolves.

Little Red Riding Hood went to visit her granny. The boy went to look after his flock of prize-winning sheep.

The boy trained his show-jumping sheep every day.

Little Red Riding Hood laughed at the boy and his jumping sheep.

One day the boy went to play a trick on her, to pay her back for laughing at him

The boy crept up behind Little
Red Riding Hood and pretended
to be a wolf. "GROWL!" he said.
"Help!" screamed Red Riding
Hood. A group of villagers
raced over.

"It was only a joke," said the shepherd boy. The villagers grumbled and walked away.

A few days later, he did it again. "GRRRRROWL!" This time Little Red Riding Hood screamed even louder. "HELLLPP!"

The villagers ran over, huffing and puffing. "It's just a joke!" the shepherd boy said.

The villagers all looked very cross.

A few days later, the boy saw
a real wolf at the door of
Granny's cottage.

"Wolf!" he shouted. But no one came. "WOLF!" he shouted, louder. Still no one came.

The boy ran over to the villagers. "Help! There's a wolf," he shouted. "Stop playing tricks," the villagers said. The boy had cried "Wolf!" too many times. Now, no one believed him.

He ran over to Granny's cottage.
The wolf was already
in Granny's bed!

"What should I do?" he thought. Then he had a brilliant idea. "SHEEP!" he cried at the top of his voice. Within seconds, his sheep were there.

"Pyramid!" shouted the boy.
The sheep jumped on each
others' shoulders.

The boy climbed up the
sheep and onto the roof.

"Sheep, follow me!" shouted the boy. He climbed inside the chimney. His sheep followed, one by one.

Inside the cottage, the wolf was licking his lips. "What big teeth you have Granny," said Red Riding Hood.

Suddenly – "THUD!" The boy fell
out the chimney and landed on
the bedroom floor. The wolf
looked up in surprise.

"Thump! Thump! Baaaa!"
A pile of sheep landed in
the fireplace.

"We're here to save you!" said
the boy. He turned to his sheep.
"Sheep, attack!" he shouted.
The sheep jumped at the wolf
and sat on top of him.

The boy and his sheep took the wolf to the villagers, who now believed his story. The shepherd boy had learned his lesson and never cried "Wolf!" again.

But you can often hear him shout "Sheep!" as he puts on a show for the villagers!

Puzzle 1

Put these pictures in the correct order.
Which event do you think is most important?
Now try writing the story in your own words!

Puzzle 2

1. We don't like liars!

2. Jumping sheep are silly!

3. I live in the woods.

4. We have been tricked!

5. I'm scared of wolves.

6. I like training sheep.

Choose the correct speech bubbles for each character. Can you think of any others? Turn over to find the answers.

Answers

Puzzle 1

The correct order is: 1e, 2a, 3f, 4c, 5d, 6b

Puzzle 2

The shepherd boy: 3, 6

Little Red Riding Hood: 2, 5

The villagers: 1, 4

Look out for more Hopscotch Twisty Tales

The Lovely Duckling
ISBN 978 1 4451 1633 4

**Hansel and Gretel
and the Green Witch**
ISBN 978 1 4451 1634 1

The Emperor's New Kit
ISBN 978 1 4451 1635 8

**Rapunzel and the
Prince of Pop**
ISBN 978 1 4451 1636 5

**Dick Whittington
Gets on his Bike**
ISBN 978 1 4451 1637 2

**The Pied Piper and
the Wrong Song**
ISBN 978 1 4451 1638 9

**The Princess and the
Frozen Peas**
ISBN 978 1 4451 0675 5

Snow White Sees the Light
ISBN 978 1 4451 0676 2

**The Elves and the
Trendy Shoes**
ISBN 978 1 4451 0678 6

The Three Frilly Goats Fluff
ISBN 978 1 4451 0677 9

Princess Frog
ISBN 978 1 4451 0679 3

Rumpled Stilton Skin
ISBN 978 1 4451 0680 9

Jack and the Bean Pie
ISBN 978 1 4451 0182 8

**Brownilocks and the Three
Bowls of Cornflakes**
ISBN 978 1 4451 0183 5

Cinderella's Big Foot
ISBN 978 1 4451 0184 2

Little Bad Riding Hood
ISBN 978 1 4451 0185 9

**Sleeping Beauty –
100 Years Later**
ISBN 978 1 4451 0186 6

**The Three Little Pigs &
the New Neighbour**
ISBN 978 1 4451 0181 1

For more Hopscotch books go to:
www.franklinwatts.co.uk